X

THE TOWN
IN THE LIBRARY

E. NESBIT

Pictures by
Shirley Tourret

Dial Books for Young Readers
NEW YORK

Rosamund and Fabian were left alone in the library. You may not believe this; but I advise you to believe everything I tell you, because it is true. Truth is stranger than storybooks, and when you grow up you will hear people say this till you grow quite sick of listening to them: you will then want to write the strangest story that ever was — just to show that *some* stories can be stranger than truth.

Mother was obliged to leave the children alone, because Nurse was ill with measles, which seems a babyish thing for a grown-up nurse to have — but it is quite true. If I had wanted to make up anything I could have said she was ill of a broken heart or a brain-fever, which always happens in books. But I wish to speak the truth even if it sounds silly. And it was measles.

Mother could not stay with the children, because it was Christmas Eve, and on that day a lot of poor old people came up to get their Christmas presents, tea and snuff, and flannel petticoats, and warm capes, and boxes of needles and cottons and things like that. Generally the children helped to give out the presents, but this year Mother was afraid they might be going to have measles themselves, and measles is a nasty forward illness with no manners at all. You can catch it from a person before they know they've got it.

So the children were left alone. Before Mother went away she said, "Look here, dears, you may play with your bricks, or make pictures with your pretty blocks that kind Uncle Thomas gave you, but you must not touch the two top drawers of the bureau. Now don't forget. And if you're good you shall have tea with me, and perhaps there will be cake. Now you *will* be good, won't you?"

2

3

Fabian and Rosamund promised faithfully that they would be *very* good and that they would not touch the two top drawers, and Mother went away to see about the flannel petticoats and the tea and snuff and tobacco and things.

When the children were left alone, Fabian said, "I am going to be very good. I shall be much more good than Mother expects me to."

"We *won't* look in the drawers," said Rosamund, stroking the shiny top of the bureau.

"We won't even *think* about the insides of the drawers," said Fabian. He stroked the bureau too and his fingers left four long streaks on it, because he had been eating toffee.

"I suppose," he said presently, "we may open the two *bottom* drawers? Mother couldn't have made a mistake — could she?"

So they opened the two bottom drawers just to be sure that Mother hadn't made a mistake, and to see whether there was anything in the bottom drawers that they ought not to look at.

But the bottom drawer of all had only old magazines in it. And the next to the bottom drawer had a lot of papers in it. The children knew at once by the look of the papers that they belonged to Father's great work about the Domestic Life of the Ancient Druids and they knew it was not right — or even interesting — to try to read other people's papers.

So they shut the drawers and looked at each other.

Fabian said, "I think it would be right to play with the bricks and pretty blocks that Uncle Thomas gave us."

But Rosamund was younger than Fabian, and she said, "I am tired of the blocks, and I am tired of Uncle Thomas. I would rather look in the drawers."

"So would I," said Fabian. And they stood looking at the bureau.

Perhaps you don't know what a bureau is — children learn very little at school nowadays — so I will tell you that a bureau is a kind of chest of drawers. Sometimes it has a bookcase on the top of it, and instead of the two little top corner drawers like the chest of drawers in a bedroom it has a sloping lid, and when it is quite open you pull out two little boards underneath — and then it makes a sort of shelf for people to write letters on. The shelf lies quite flat, and lets you see little drawers inside with mother-of-pearl handles — and a row of pigeon holes — (which are not holes pigeons live in, but places for keeping the letters carrier-pigeons could carry round their necks if they liked). And there is very often a tiny cupboard in the middle of the bureau, with a pattern on the door in different coloured woods. So now you know.

Fabian stood first on one leg and then on the other, till Rosamund said, "Well, you might as well pull up your socks."

So he did. His socks were always just like a concertina or a very expensive photographic camera, but he used to say it was not his fault, and I suppose he knew best.

Then he said, "I say, Rom! Mother only said we weren't to *touch* the two top drawers."

"I *should* like to be good," said Rosamund.

"I *mean* to be good," said Fabian. "But if you took the little thin poker that is not kept for best you could put it through one of the brass handles and I could hold the other handle with the tongs. And then we could open the drawer without touching it."

"So we could! How clever you are, Fabe," said Rosamund. And she admired her brother very much. So they took the poker and the tongs. The front of the bureau got a little scratched, but the top drawer came open, and there they saw two boxes with glass tops and narrow gold paper going all round; though you could only see paper shavings through the glass they knew

it was soldiers. Besides these boxes there was a doll and a donkey standing on a green grass plot that had wooden wheels, and a little wickerwork doll's cradle, and some brass cannons, and a bag that looked like marbles, and some flags, and a mouse that seemed as though it moved with clockwork; only, of course, they had promised not to touch the drawer, so they could not make sure. They looked at each other, and Fabian said:

"I wish it was tomorrow!"

You have seen that Fabian was quite a clever boy; and he knew at once that these were the Christmas presents which Santa Claus had brought for him and Rosamund. But Rosamund said, "Oh dear, I wish we hadn't!"

However, she consented to open the other drawer —
without touching it, of course, because she promised
faithfully — and when, with the poker and tongs, the
other drawer came open, there were large wooden boxes
— the kind that hold raisins and figs — and round
boxes with paper on — smooth on the top and folded in
pleats round the edge; and the children knew what was
inside without looking. Everyone knows what candied fruit looks like on the
outside of the box. There were square boxes, too — the kind that have
crackers in — with a cracker going off on the lid, very different in size and
brightness from what it does really, for, as no doubt you know, a cracker very
often comes in two quite calmly, without any pop at all, and then you only
have the motto and the sweet, which is never nice. Of course, if there is
anything else in the cracker, such as brooches or rings, you have to let the
little girl who sits next to you at supper have it.

When they had pushed back the drawer Fabian said, "Let us pull out
the writing drawer and make a castle."

So they pulled the drawer out and put it on the
floor. Please do not try to do this if your father has a
bureau, because it leads to trouble. It was only
because this one was broken that they were able
to do it. Then they began to build.

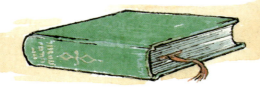

11

They had the two boxes of bricks — the wooden bricks with the pillars and the coloured glass windows, and the rational bricks which are made of clay like tiles. When all the bricks were used up they got the pretty picture blocks that kind Uncle Thomas gave them, and they built with these; but one box of blocks does not go far.

Picture blocks are only good for building, except just at first. When you have made the pictures a few times you know exactly how they go, and then what's the good? This is a fault which belongs to many very expensive toys. These blocks had six pictures — Windsor Castle with the Royal Standard hoisted; ducks in a pond, with a very handsome green and blue drake; the King in his robes; a snowball fight — but none of the boys knew how to chuck a snowball; the Harvest Festival; and the Death of Nelson.

These did not go far, as I said. There are six times as few blocks as there are pictures, because every block has six sides. If you don't understand this it shows they don't teach arithmetic at your school, or else that you don't do your home lessons.

But the best of a library is the books. Rosamund and Fabian made up with books. They got Shakespeare in fourteen volumes, and Rollin's *Ancient History* and Gibbon's *Decline and Fall*, and the *Beauties of Literature* in fifty-six fat little volumes, and they built not only a castle, but a town — and a big town — that presently towered high above them on the top of the bureau.

"It's almost big enough to get into," said Fabian, "if we had some steps." So they made steps with the *Spectator* and the *Rambler*, and the *Observer*, and the *Tatler*; and when the steps were done they walked up them.

12

You may think that they could not have walked up these steps and into a town they had built themselves, but I assure you people have often done it, and anyway this is a true story. They had made a lovely gateway with two fat volumes of old poetical works on top, and as they went through it they felt all the feelings which people have to feel when they are tourists and see really fine architecture. (Architecture means buildings, but it is a grander word, as you see.)

Rosamund and Fabian simply walked up the steps into the town they had built. Whether they got smaller or the town got larger, I do not pretend to say. When they had gone under the great gateway they found that they were in a street which they could not remember building. But they were not disagreeable about it, and they said it was a very nice street all the same.

There was a large square in the middle of the town, with seats, and there they sat down, in the town they had made, and wondered how they could have been so clever as to build it. Then they went to the walls of the town — high, strong walls built of the *Encyclopaedia* and the *Biographical Dictionary* — and far away over the brown plain of the carpet they saw a great thing like a square mountain. It was very shiny. And as they looked at it a great slice of it pushed itself out, and Fabian saw the brass handles shine, and he said:

''Why, Rom, that's the bureau.''

''It's larger than I want it to be,'' said Rosamund, who was a little frightened. And indeed it did seem to be an extra size, for it was higher than the town.

The drawer of the great mountain bureau opened slowly, and the children could see something moving inside; then they saw the glass lid of one of the boxes go slowly up till it stood on end and looked like one side of the Crystal Palace, it was so large — and inside the box they saw something moving. The shavings and tissue-paper and the cotton-wool heaved and tossed like a sea when it is rough and you wish you had not come for a sail. And then from among the heaving whiteness came out a blue soldier, and another and another. They let themselves down from the drawer with ropes of shavings, and when they were all out there were fifty of them — foot soldiers with rifles and fixed bayonets, as well as a thin captain on a horse and a sergeant and a drummer.

The drummer beat his drum and the whole company formed fours and

16

marched straight for the town. They seemed to be quite full-size soldiers —
indeed, extra large.

The children were very frightened. They left the walls and ran up and
down the streets of the town trying to find a place to hide.

"Oh, there's our very own house," cried Rosamund at last; "we shall be
safe there." She was surprised as well as pleased to find their own house inside
the town they had built.

So they ran in, and into the library, and there was the bureau and the town
they had built, and it was all small and quite the proper size. But when they
looked out of the window it was not their own street, but the one they had
built; they could see two volumes of the *Beauties of Literature* and the head of
the King in the house opposite, and down the street was the mausoleum they
had built after the pattern given in the red and yellow book that went with
the bricks. It was all very confusing.

Suddenly, as they stood looking out of the windows, they heard a shouting, and there were the blue soldiers coming along the street by twos, and when the Captain got opposite their house he called out, "Fabian! Rosamund! Come down!"

And they had to, for they were very much frightened.

Then the Captain said, "We have taken this town, and you are our prisoners. Do not attempt to escape, or I don't know what will happen to you."

The children explained that they had built the town, so they thought it was theirs; but the Captain said very politely, "That doesn't follow at all. It's our town now. And I want provisions for my soldiers."

"We haven't any," said Fabian, but Rosamund nudged him, and said, "Won't the soldiers be very fierce if they are hungry?"

The Blue Captain heard her, and said, "You are quite right, little girl. If you have any food, produce it. It will be a generous act, and may stop any unpleasantness. My soldiers *are* very fierce. Besides," he added in a lower tone, speaking behind his hand, "you need only feed the soldiers in the usual way."

When the children heard this their minds were made up.

"If you do not mind waiting a minute," said Fabian, politely, "I will bring down any little things I can find."

Then he took his tongs, and Rosamund took the poker, and they opened the drawer where the raisins and figs and dried fruits were — for everything in the library in the town was just the same as in the library at home — and they carried them out into the big square where the Captain had drawn up his blue regiment. And here the soldiers were fed. I suppose you know how tin soldiers are fed? But children learn so little at school nowadays that I daresay you don't, so I will tell you. You just put a bit of fig or raisin, or whatever it is, on the soldier's tin bayonet — or his sword, if he is a cavalry man — and you let it stay on till you are tired of playing at giving the soldiers rations and then of course you eat it for him. This was the way in which Fabian and Rosamund fed the starving blue soldiers. But when they had done so, the

soldiers were as hungry as ever.

So then the Blue Captain, who had not had anything, even on the point of his sword, said, "More, more, my gallant men are fainting for lack of food."

So there was nothing for it but to bring out the candied fruits, and to feed the soldiers with them. So Fabian and Rosamund stuck bits of candied apricot and fig and pear and cherry and beetroot on the tops of the soldiers' bayonets, and when every soldier had a piece they put a fat candied cherry on the officer's sword. Then the children knew the soldiers would be quiet for a few minutes, and they ran back into their own house and into the library to talk to each other about what they had better do, for they both felt that the blue soldiers were a very hardhearted set of men.

"They might shut us up in the dungeons," said Rosamund, "and then Mother might lock us in, when she shut up the lid of the bureau, and we should starve to death."

"I think it's all nonsense," said Fabian. But when they looked out of the window there was the house with Windsor Castle and the head of the King just opposite.

"If we could only find Mother," said Rosamund; but they knew without looking that Mother was not in the house that they were in then.

"I wish we had that mouse that looked like clockwork, and the donkey, and the other box of soldiers — perhaps they are red ones, and they would fight the blue and lick them; because redcoats are English and they always win," said Fabian.

And then Rosamund said, "Oh, Fabe, I believe we could go into *this* town, too, if we tried!"

So they went to the bureau drawer, and Rosamund got out the other box of soldiers and the mouse — it *was* a clockwork one — and the donkey with panniers, and put them in the town, while Fabian ate up a few odd raisins they had dropped on the floor.

When all the soldiers (they were *red*) were arranged on the ramparts of the little town, Fabian said, "I'm sure we can get into this town," and sure enough they did, just as they had done into the first one. And it was exactly the same sort of town as the other.

So now they were in a town built in a library in a house in a town built in a library in a house in a town called London — and the town they were in now had red soldiers in it and they felt quite safe, and the Union Jack was stuck up over the gateway. It was a stiff little flag they had found with some others in the bureau drawer; it was meant to be stuck in Christmas pudding, but they had stuck it between two blocks and put it over the gate of their town. They walked about this town and found their own house, just as before, and went in, and there was the toy town on the floor; and you will see that they might have walked into that town also, but they saw that it was no good, and that they couldn't get out that way, but would only get deeper and deeper into a nest of towns in libraries in houses in towns in libraries in houses in towns in . . . and so on for always — something like Chinese puzzle-boxes multiplied by millions and millions for ever and ever. And they did not like even to think of this, because of course they would be getting further and further from home every time. And when Fabian explained all this to Rosamund she said he made

her head ache, and she began to cry.

Then Fabian thumped her on the back and told her not to be a little silly, for he was a very kind brother. And he said, "Come out and let's see if the soldiers can tell us what to do."

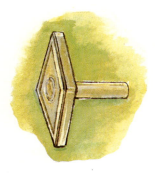

So they went out; but the red soldiers said they knew nothing but drill, and even the Red Captain said he really couldn't advise. Then they met the clockwork mouse. He was big like an elephant, and the donkey with panniers was as big as a mastodon or a megatherium. (If they teach you anything at school of course they have taught you all about the megatherium and the mastodon.)

The mouse kindly stopped to speak to the children, and Rosamund burst into tears again and said she wanted to go home.

The great mouse looked down at her and said, "I am sorry for *you*, but your brother is the kind of child that overwinds clockwork mice the very first day he has them. I prefer to stay this size, and you to stay small."

Then Fabian said: "On my honour, I won't. If we get back home I'll give you to Rosamund. That is, supposing I get you for one of my Christmas presents."

The donkey with panniers said, "And you won't put coals in my panniers or unglue my feet from my green grass-plot because I look more natural without wheels?"

"I give you my word," said Fabian, "I wouldn't think of such a thing."

"Very well," said the mouse, "then I will tell you. It is a great secret, but there is only one way to get out of this kind of town. You — I hardly know how to explain — you — you just walk out of the gate, you know."

"Dear me," said Rosamund; "I never thought of that!"

So they all went to the gate of the town and walked out, and there they were in the library again. But when they looked out of the window the Mausoleum was still to be seen, and the terrible blue soldiers.

"What are we to do now?" asked Rosamund; but the clockwork mouse and the donkey with panniers were their proper size again now (or else the children had got bigger. It is no use asking me which, for I do not know), and so of course they could not speak.

"We must walk out of this town as we did out of the other," said Fabian.

"Yes," Rosamund said, "only this town is full of blue soldiers and I am afraid of them. Don't you think it would do if we *ran* out?"

28

So out they ran and down the steps that were made of the *Spectator* and the *Rambler* and the *Tatler* and the *Observer*. And directly they stood on the brown library carpet they ran to the window and looked out, and they saw — instead of the building with Windsor Castle and the King's head in it — they saw their own road with the trees without any leaves and the man was just going along lighting the lamps with the stick that the gas-light pops out of like a bird, to roost in the glass cage at the top of the lamppost. So they knew that they were safe at home again.

And as they stood looking out they heard the library door open, and Mother's voice saying, "What a dreadful muddle! And what have you done with the raisins and the candied fruits?" And her voice was very grave indeed.

Now you will see that it was quite impossible for Fabian and Rosamund to explain to their mother what they had done with the raisins and things, and how they had been in a town in a library in a house in a town they had built in their own library with the books and the bricks and the pretty picture blocks kind Uncle Thomas gave them. Because they were much younger than I am, and even I have found it rather hard to explain.

So Rosamund said, "Oh, Mother, my head does ache so," and began to cry. And Fabian said nothing, but he, also, began to cry.

And Mother said, "I don't wonder your head aches, after all those sweet things." And she looked as if she would like to cry too.

"I don't know what Daddy will say," said Mother, and then she gave them each a nasty powder and put them both to bed.

"I wonder what he *will* say," said Fabian just before he went to sleep.

"*I* don't know," said Rosamund, and, strange to say, they don't know to this hour what Daddy said. Because next day they both had measles, and when they got better everyone had forgotten about what had happened on Christmas Eve. And Fabian and Rosamund had forgotten just as much as everybody else. So I should never have heard of it but for the clockwork mouse. It was he who told me the story, just as the children told it to him in the town in the library in the house in the town they built in their own library with the books and the bricks and the pretty picture blocks which were given to them by kind Uncle Thomas. And if you do not believe the story it is not my fault: I believe every word the mouse said, for I know the good character of that clockwork mouse, and I know it could not tell an untruth even if it tried.

30

First published in the United States 1988
by Dial Books for Young Readers
A Division of NAL Penguin Inc.
2 Park Avenue
New York, New York 10016

Published in Great Britain by Beehive Books,
an imprint of Macdonald & Company (Publishers) Limited
© This edition Macdonald & Company (Publishers) Limited 1987
Printed and bound in Spain by Novograph, S.A., Madrid
First Edition
US
1 3 5 7 9 10 8 6 4 2

Library of Congress Cataloging in Publication Data

Nesbit, E. [Edith]. 1858-1924. The town in the library.

Summary: Playing in the library of their home.
Rosamund and Fabian build a huge town out of books,
only to find themselves trapped there when they go inside.
[1. Fantasy] I. Tourret, Shirley, ill. II. Title
PZ7.N43777To 1988   [Fic]   87-8971
ISBN 0-8037-0477-1